D1179359

The House that JACK Built

Scholastic Children's Books,
Commonwealth House, 1-19 New Oxford Street,
London WC1A 1NU, UK
a division of Scholastic Ltd

London ~ New York ~ Toronto ~ Sydney ~ Auckland
Mexico City ~ New Delhi ~ Hong Kong

Text and illustrations copyright © Elena Gomez 2001

ISBN 0 439 99234 6

Printed and bound in China

The House that JACK Built

Elena Gomez

SCHOLASTIC
PRESS

This is the HOUSE that Jack built.

This is the MALT

that lay in the house that Jack built.

This is the RAT that ate the malt

that lay in the house
that Jack built.

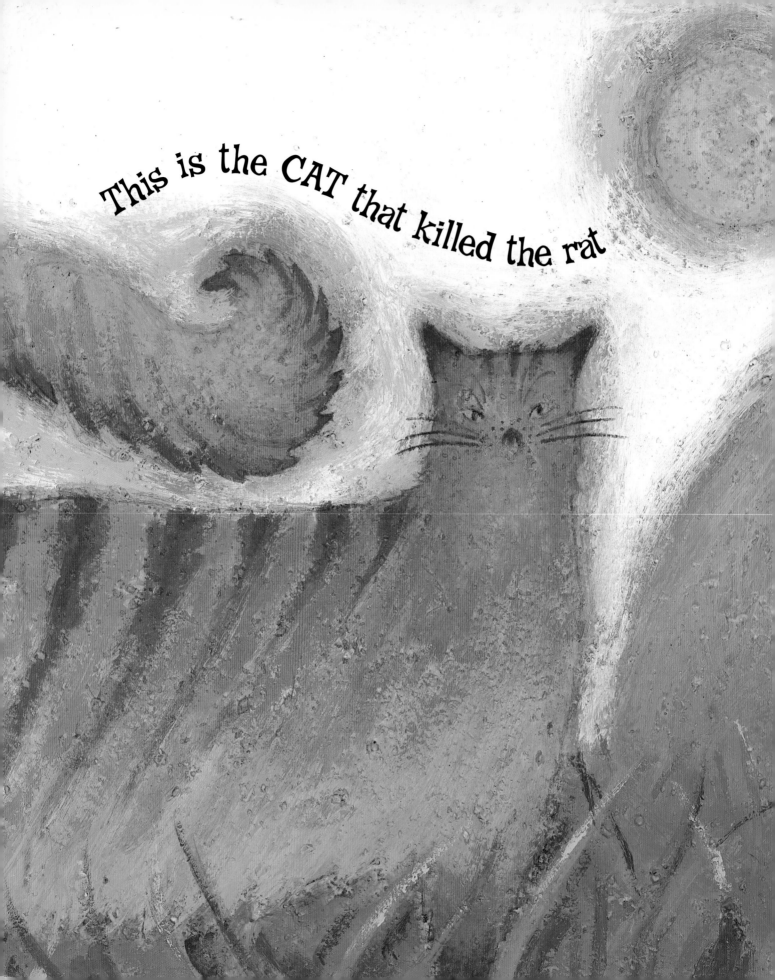

This is the CAT that killed the rat

that ate the malt that lay in the house
that Jack built.

This is the DOG that worried the cat that killed the rat that ate the malt

that lay in the house that Jack built.

This is the COW
with the crumpled horn

that tossed the dog

that worried the cat

that killed the rat

that ate the malt

that lay in the house that Jack built.

This is the MAIDEN all forlorn

that milked the cow with the crumpled horn
that tossed the dog that worried the cat
that killed the rat that ate the malt that lay
in the house that Jack built.

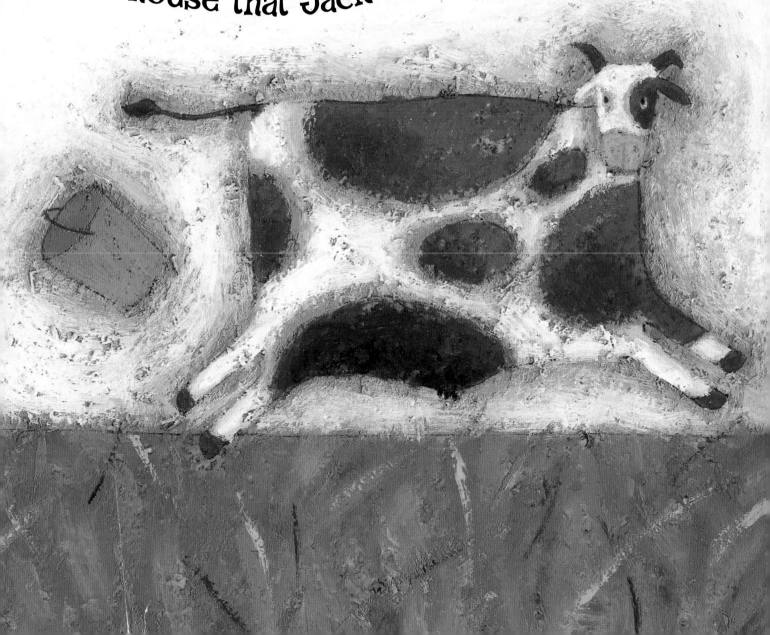

that milked the cow with the crumpled horn
that tossed the dog that worried the cat
that killed the rat that ate the malt that
lay in the house that Jack built.

This is the PRIEST all shaven and shorn

that married the man all tattered and torn
that kissed the maiden all forlorn that
milked the cow with the crumpled horn that
tossed the dog that worried the cat that
killed the rat that ate the malt that lay in the
house that Jack built.

This is the COCK that crowed in the morn

that woke the priest all shaven and shorn that married the man all tattered and torn that kissed the maiden all forlorn that milked the cow with the crumpled horn that tossed the dog that worried the cat that killed the rat that ate the malt that lay in the house that Jack built.

This is the FARMER sewing his corn
that kept the cock that crowed in the morn

that woke the priest all shaven and shorn

that married the man all tattered and torn

that kissed the maiden all forlorn . . .

... that milked the cow with the crumpled horn

that tossed the dog that worried the cat
that killed the rat that
ate the malt that lay
in the house that
Jack built.

This is the HORSE and the HOUND
at dawn that belonged to the
farmer sewing his corn

that kept the cock that crowed in the morn
that woke the priest all shaven and shorn that
married the man all tattered and torn . . .

...that kissed the maiden all forlorn

that milked the cow with the crumpled horn
that tossed the dog that worried the cat
that killed the rat that ate the malt that
lay in the house . . .

. . . that JACK built!